-to-GOODNESS truth

PATRICIA C. McKISSACK
GISELLE POTTER

ALADDIN PAPERBACKS
New York London Toronto Sydney Singapore

to JOHN FiTzPATRiCK McKiSSACK
— P. C. M.

FOR ChLOË
— G. P.

First Aladdin Paperbacks edition January 2003

Text copyright © 2000 by Patricia C. McKissack
Illustrations copyright © 2000 by Giselle Potter

ALADDIN PAPERBACKS
An imprint of Simon & Schuster
Children's Publishing Division
1230 Avenue of the Americas
New York, NY 10020

Also available in an Atheneum Books for Young Readers hardcover edition.
Designed by Angela Carlino
The text of this book was set in Joanna Semi Bold.
The illustrations are rendered in pencil, ink, gouache, gesso, and watercolor.

Manufactured in China
11

The Library of Congress has cataloged the hardcover edition as follows:
McKissack, Patricia C., 1944-
The honest-to-goodness truth / by Patricia C. McKissack; illustrated by Giselle Potter.—1st ed.
p. cm.
"An Anne Schwartz book."
Summary: After promising never to lie, Libby learns it's not always necessary to blurt out the whole truth either.
ISBN 0-689-82668-0 (hc)
[1. Honesty—Fiction. 2. Conduct of life—Fiction.] I. Potter, Giselle, ill. II. Title.
PZ7.M478693Ho 2000 [E]—dc21 98-47070
ISBN 0-689-85395-5 (pbk.)

Libby hurried out the door and down the porch steps. "Did you feed and water Ol' Boss?" Mama called from her sewing room window.

Libby stopped at the gate. "Yes, Mama," she answered. She was surprised at how easy the lie slid out of her mouth, like it was greased with warm butter.

Mama stopped sewing Virginia Washington's wedding dress and came outside. Libby dropped her head and wouldn't look in her mother's eyes. "Are you sure?" Mama asked real stern-like. "Speak the truth and shame the devil."

Libby opened her mouth, but Mama placed a finger in the air as a signal for her to stop. "Libby Louise Sullivan, I'll ask you once more and again: Did you feed and water Ol' Boss?"

Libby's stomach felt like she'd swallowed a handful of chicken feathers. Her eyes commenced to fill with water and her bottom lip quivered. Then, taking a deep breath and gulping hard, she owned up to her lie. "I was gon' do it soon as I got back from jumping rope with Ruthie Mae."

Libby felt a lot better, even though Mama punished her double. For not tending to Ol' Boss, Libby couldn't go play with Ruthie Mae. And for lying, she had to stay on the porch the rest of the day. It was the first time Libby had lied to Mama, and as far as she was concerned it was gon' be the last. "From now on, only the truth," she decided.

Libby started her truth-telling come Sunday morning.

All the children from Briarsville were gathered outside the small church, waiting on Sunday school to begin. Everybody was admiring Ruthie Mae's new dress and matching hat when Libby came skipping up. "Morning, everybody. Morning, Ruthie Mae," she spoke all nice. "I like your outfit. It's real pretty . . . but you've got a hole in your sock."

All eyes went from the hat to the dress to the hole. Meanwhile, Libby skipped up the steps and inside the church without ever noticing the hurt on her best friend's face.

Service ended and, same as always, Libby asked Ruthie Mae to
walk home. "No, no, and no again!" Ruthie Mae glared at her.
Libby was purely surprised. "What'd I do?"
"You told the world I had a hole in my sock."
"It was the truth," Libby pronounced, feeling satisfied.
"It was plain mean!" replied Ruthie Mae, and she hurried away.

Libby looked at the idea from the outside in, and then from the inside out as she walked home alone. By the time she trudged up her steps, she was still confused.

The next morning, Libby joined a group of friends on the way to school.

"Did you do your geography homework?" Willie asked Libby.

"It was easy," she answered.

"Not for me." Willie shook his head. "I didn't understand it, so I didn't do it."

First thing in class, Libby started waving her hand. "Me, Miz Jackson, me, me, me, Miz Jackson!" When the teacher called on her, Libby announced, "Willie don't got his geography homework."

"Doesn't have his homework," corrected Miz Jackson.

"No, ma'am, he don't." Libby was pleased with herself.

Willie gave her an ugly look. "Why'd you tell on me?" he whispered as he headed to Miz Jackson's desk to explain.

With certainty she whispered back, "All I did was tell it like it is. So there!" And she folded her hands neatly in her lap.

Before lunchtime, Libby had told a lot of truths. She reminded everybody how Daisy had forgotten her Christmas speech and cried in front of all the parents.

She told how Charlesetta had gotten a spanking for stealing peaches off Miz Stacey's tree.

And the whole class knew that Thomas didn't have lunch money and had to borrow some from Miz Jackson.

By the time school was out, hardly anyone would talk to her.

"Why are y'all so mad at me?" Libby asked as her classmates started home without her.

On Libby's way home, she wondered why her stomach felt as fluttery as it did when she'd told the lie. "I promised Mama I would tell the truth no matter how much it hurt," she reassured herself glumly. "And that's all I done."

Before Libby knew it, she was in front of Miz Tusselbury's vine-covered cottage. The woman was in her rocking chair, gliding back and forward and fanning herself with a hand-folded fan. "How-do, Libby Louise," she called in her sing-song voice. "What's that sad look you wearing on such a pretty day?"

Libby jumped right in with what was bothering her. "Can the truth be wrong?"

"Oh, no," Miz Tusselbury said, fanning faster. "The truth is never wrong. Always, always tell the truth!"

"That's what I thought," Libby said, a smile of relief lighting up her face.

Miz Tusselbury leaned over the railing to pluck a bloom from one of the vines that grew all over her yard and up her house. "Don't you think my garden is lovely?"

Libby thought on it. Ordinarily she would have just said yes, for fear of sounding sassy. But that wasn't the truth. So polite as you please, she answered, "Miz Tusselbury, truly and honestly, your yard looks like a . . . a . . . a jungle."

"Well, I declare!" Miz Tusselbury gasped.

"Don't be mad!" Libby pleaded.

But it was too late. Miz Tusselbury rushed inside her house and slammed the door.

Even though Mama was busy putting the finishing touches on Virginia Washington's wedding dress, she still took time to listen to Libby's problem.

"I feel something awful. My friends don't like me no more."

"Any more," repeated her mother.

"No, they don't—and just 'cause I told the truth." The girl sighed deeply.

Handing her a needle to thread, Mama asked gently, "Are you sure they're mad at you for telling the truth?"

"I think so," said Libby. "Willie was mad as a hornet when I told Miz Jackson he didn't have his homework. And Miz Tusselbury got plenty upset when I said her garden looked like a jungle."

Mama smiled. "Oh, I see." Then, putting down her work, she took Libby's hands, saying, "Sometimes the truth is told at the wrong time or in the wrong way, or for the wrong reasons. And that can be hurtful. But the honest-to-goodness truth is never wrong." Then Mama went back to stitching and pulling, stitching and pulling.

Libby walked to the barn to feed and water Ol' Boss, all the time trying to get an understanding of her mother's words. Just then Virginia Washington sashayed out of the fields and past the barn—come for the final fitting of her wedding dress.

As she watched Libby brush Ol' Boss, Virginia burst into laughter. "That horse is older than black pepper," she said, shaking her head. "I doubt you could get a dollar for that old flea-ridden swayback." And she flounced off toward the house.

"Don't say those things about Ol' Boss," Libby called after her, throwing her arms around the horse's neck. She knew he wasn't the fine carriage horse he had once been, but why did Virginia have to rub it in?

Now Libby thought back on her own truth-telling, and Mama's words suddenly became crystal clear.

The next day, Libby caught up with her friends on the way to school. She told Ruthie Mae, "You did have a hole in your sock, but I could have whispered it to you instead of hollering it out for everybody to hear. I'm sorry."

Ruthie Mae smiled. "You finally got it," she said.

Libby apologized to Willie, too. "I should have let you tell Miz Jackson 'bout your own homework. It was unfair. Besides, nobody asked me in the first place."

"That's alright. But, hey," he added, "do you think you could help me with my geography homework?"

"No problem," said Libby.

Later, Libby talked to all the other victims of her truth-telling.

But there was one more person she had to see. On the way home, she headed straight for Miz Tusselbury's house.

Libby found her neighbor out front, down on all fours, pulling up flowers and snatching up vines by the roots. When Miz Tusselbury saw her, she wiped her brow with the back of her hand and flashed a full smile.

"I'm sorry if I hurt your feelings yesterday," Libby said.

"Libby Louise, you were right," Miz Tusselbury replied. "This place had gone completely and uncontrollably wild!"

"But you were so mad at me."

Miz Tusselbury waved a dismissing hand. "The truth is often hard to chew. But if it is sweetened with love, then it is a little easier to swallow."

Libby really did understand. She picked up a hoe and began helping.
"Things are really looking pretty good around here," she said. And that
was the honest-to-goodness truth.

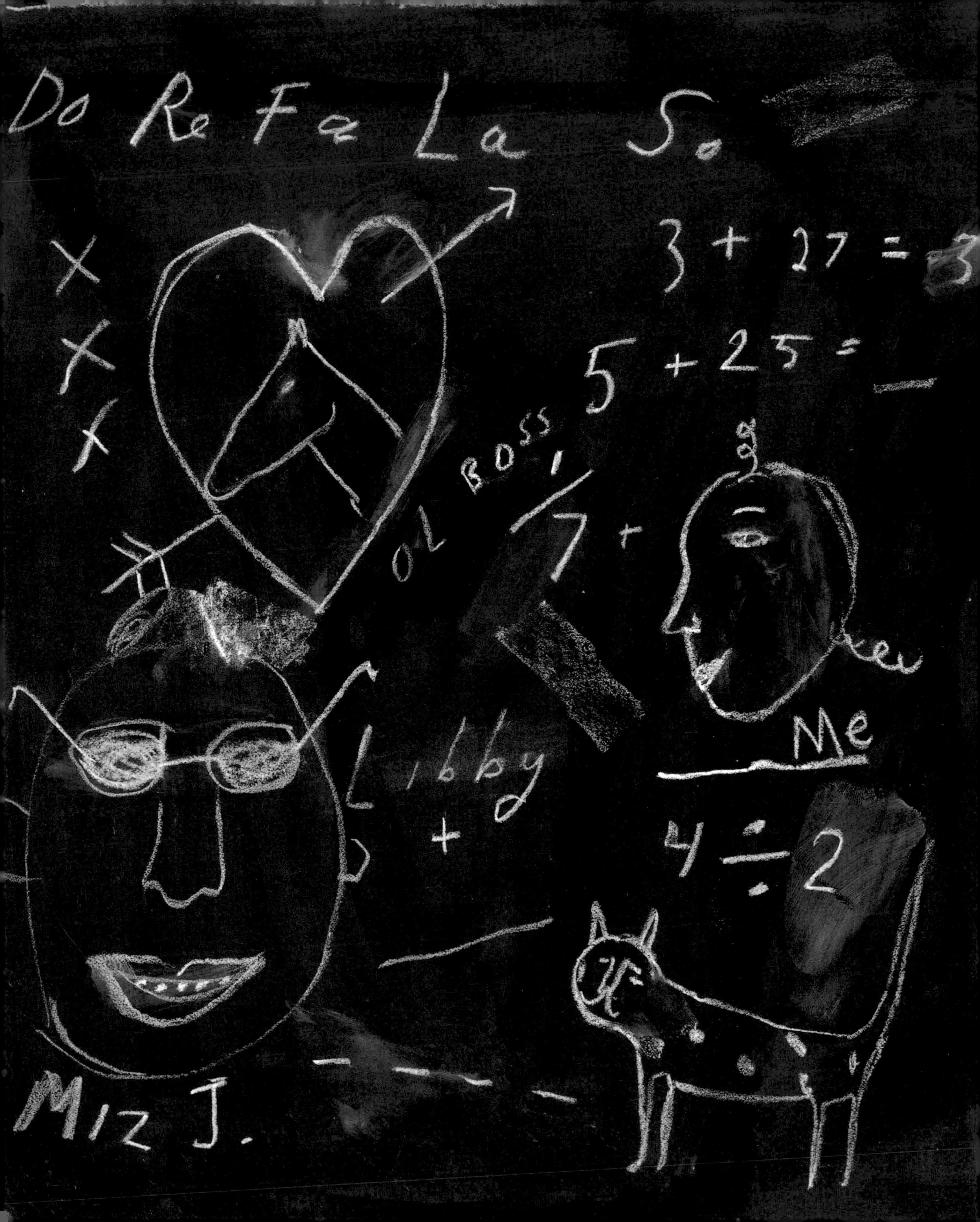
Do Re Fa La So
3 + 27 = 3
5 + 25 = ___
OL BOSS
7 +
Me
Libby
+
4 ÷ 2
MIZ J.